JAMAICA SANDWICH?

JAMAICA SANDWICH?

by BRIAN P. CLEARY

illustrated by
RICK DUPRÉ

LERNER PUBLICATIONS COMPANY / MINNEAPOLIS

Library of Congress Cataloging-in-Publication Data

Cleary, Brian P., 1959–
    Jamaica sandwich? / by Brian P. Cleary ; illustrated by Rick Dupré.
      p. cm.
    Summary : A humorous rhyming tale, filled with puns based on geographical names.
    ISBN 0–8225–2114–8
    1. Family—Fiction. 2. Animals—Fiction. [1. Geography—Fiction. 2. Puns and punning—Fiction. 3. Stories in rhyme.] I. Dupré, Rick, ill. II. Title.
PZ8.3.C555Jam 1996
[Fic]—dc20   94–39913

Manufactured in the United States of America
1 2 3 4 5 6 – I/JR – 01 00 99 98 97 96

For my parents, Mike and Sue, who never
doubted they'd raise a bookmaker
B.P.C.

For my sister Mary Beth, who taught me
how to draw curly hair
R.D.

"Jamaica **SANDWICH**?" Grandma asked,
and I replied I ate
some **CHILE** from a China bowl
and TURKEY from a plate.

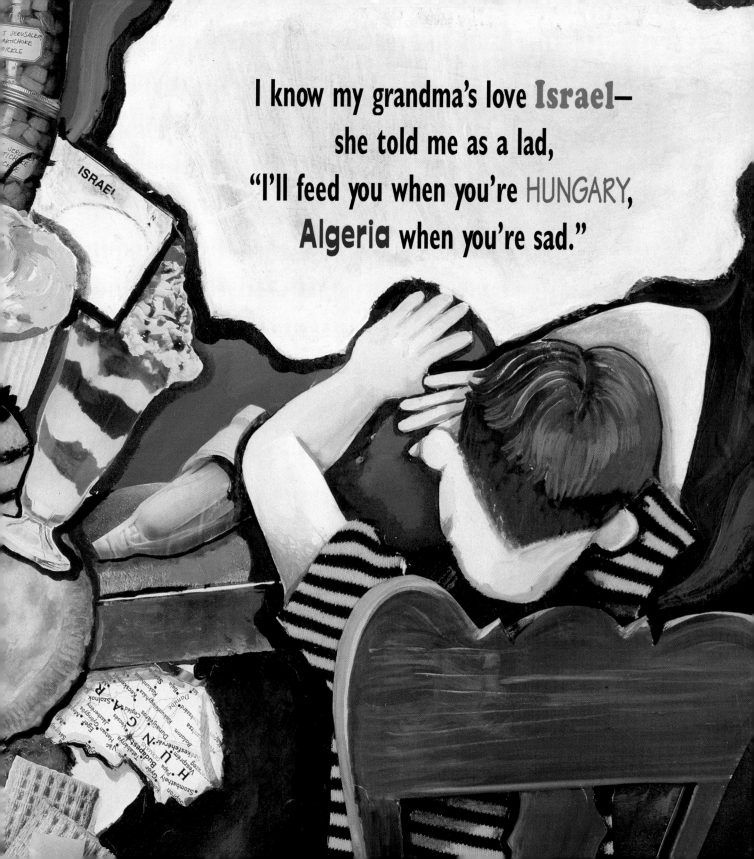

I know my grandma's love Israel—
she told me as a lad,
"I'll feed you when you're HUNGARY,
Algeria when you're sad."

IRAN and played at Grandpa's farm,
GREENLAND so plush and full—
I fed the pigs and milked the cows
and rode on **Istanbul**.

BEIRUT, LEBANON

Population.................................
Lifetime B.A...................1,100,000
Lifetime R.B.I.....................342
Home Runs........................2211
Candy Bars.........................714

BABE

As a **SYRIA** scholar of baseball,
my grandpa has often professed,
"Of all the men who ever played,
Beirut is still the best."

"U.S. me how's your singing,"
said Aunt Anna as I bowed.
"Juneau, my boy, you SINGAPORE,
but my, you sure sing loud!"

Aunt Anna can fix anything—
a **PARIS** skates, a cup.
If your pants rip Indonesia
just **HAVANA** sew 'em up.

I **Russia** round on my red bike
and feel **NEW ZEALAND** vigor
when I take a kite and **Taiwan** on
and sail my ten-speed rigger.

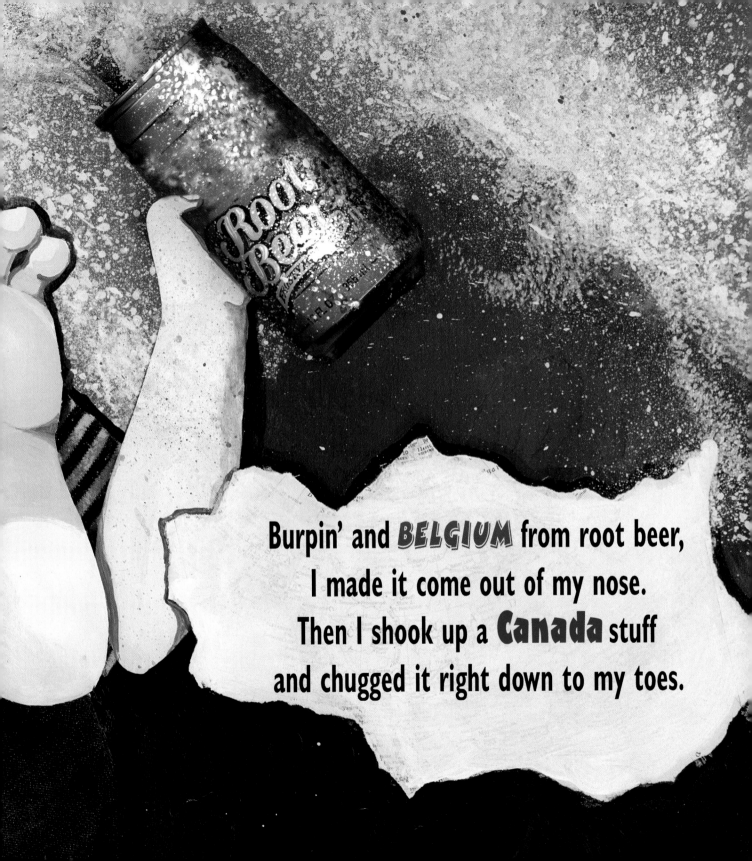

Burpin' and **BELGIUM** from root beer,
I made it come out of my nose.
Then I shook up a **Canada** stuff
and chugged it right down to my toes.

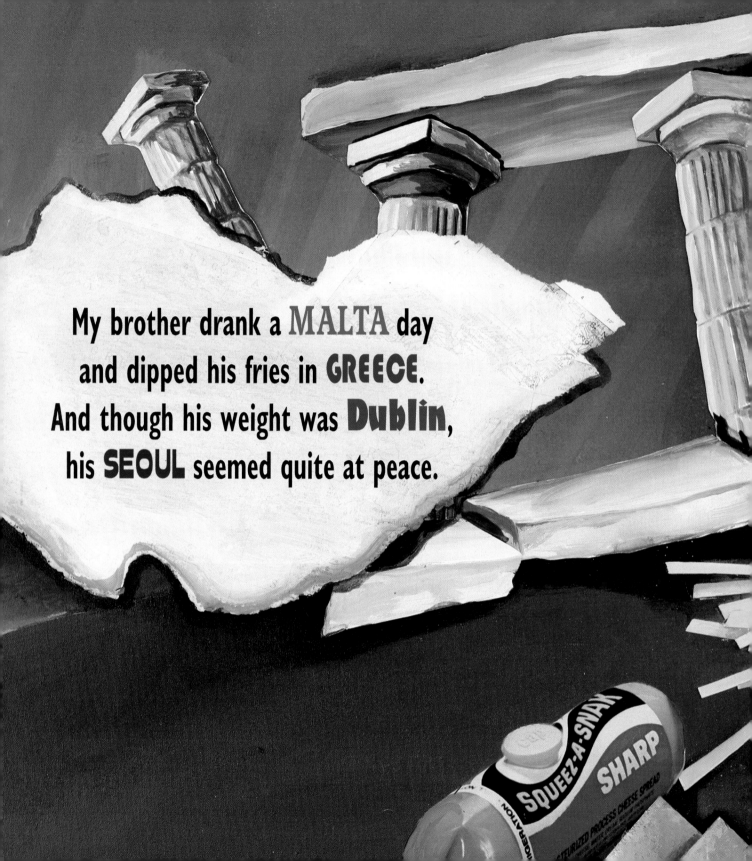

He started using Sweden low
and working off his belly.
But then the LAOS got VATICAN
when they opened that New Delhi.

We went out to the racetrack,
Kenya tell why I'm upset?
I picked out all the winners
but my dad's too cheap **TIBET**!

My dad comes home so tired
he can't keep his Bering Strait.
His Sudan THAILAND on the floor,
his shoes land on his plate.

"EUROPE too late," my grandma said.
"Uganda get some sleep.
Lie down in bed and count some WALES."
(I think that she meant sheep.)

Geography Test

A+

1. If you ate **Chile,** what continent would get smaller? South America

2. **Kenya** name the capital of **Kenya**? Nairobi

3. **Uganda** know, on which continent is the country of **Uganda**? Africa

4. If **Wales** were swimming in your bathtub, what neighbor would report it lost? England

5. If you are feeling **New Zealand** vigor, which hemisphere are you in? the Southern Hemisphere

6. When you need to find a **Paris** skates, what country should you visit? France

7. Write a geography pun of your own.